Birth
of a
Ninja

Peter Marney

Copyright © 2017 Peter Marney

All rights reserved

This book is a work of fiction. The names, characters, places and incidents are products of the writer's imagination or have been used fictitiously and are not to be construed as real.

Any resemblance to persons, living or dead, actual events, locales or organisations is entirely coincidental.

ISBN-13: 978-1973902461

ISBN-10: 197390246X

This book is dedicated to my family without whom none of this would be possible.

Read this first

You are not a ninja.

It's very important that you keep remembering this.

If you try to copy any of the stuff in this book then you might end up in hospital.

Even if you copy just some of this stuff, you'll end up in trouble.

This will be bad.

This will be very bad because I'll get the blame.

So please, remember you're not a ninja and promise not to try and copy me.

Have you promised?

Ok, you can now read on.

Enter the Hero

Bum!

"Stay out of trouble," Mum said.

So, what am I doing?

Sorry Mum.

I'm Jamie by the way and I'm just about to get into a fight.

I blame Dad.

Before he left, he used to let me watch his Kung Fu films and I got the idea that I could be an action hero. A wandering ninja swordsman with these amazing fighting skills.

So here I am, trying to stop two big lads picking on a girl and I haven't even got to school yet.

"What d'you want?" says the chubby one.

"Maybe he wants what she's getting," says the other, the joker of the two.

I try to look taller.

"Maybe she wants to be somewhere else," I say.

I know that's what I want.

I want to be somewhere else, probably at home and maybe even hiding under my bed.

They both turn towards me.

"So, what you going to do about it then?"

I could have walked away.

I should have walked away.

But that isn't what a ninja hero does, is it?

A ninja hero reaches for his sword and, in a blur of action, kills the bad guys and saves the girl.

Shame I don't have a sword.

As the bullies come towards me I take up the Fighting Tiger stance, the fiercest looking move I can remember.

Someone's about to get hurt.

Trouble is, that someone's me.

All I know about Kung Fu is from watching the telly. I've never had a fight in my life until now and I don't think this is going to end well.

Peter Marney

A stranger

Suddenly the bullies freeze.

My scary face and Fighting Tiger pose has made them think twice about hitting me!

That's when the girl starts to grin.

What's she grinning at?

It's not funny from where I'm standing.

Then I hear the voice behind me.

"Hello lads. Nice of you to look after my cousin on her way to school. That was what you were doing wasn't it?"

Well, at least someone sounds friendly.

The bullies nod quickly, still frozen to the spot. If they're scared then maybe I should start getting worried too.

"Well," the voice says, "I think she can manage from here, so why don't you run along?"

The bullies start to move.

"But if any accidents happen to these two, then I'm going to come looking for you. Understand?"

They nod even faster.

"Right, now RUN!"

They can run fast for big lads.

That's left just the three of us.

"What's the story with this one Red?" the voice asks. "You know him?"

Well, at least I know her name now, though I suppose I could have guessed it anyway what with the ginger hair.

"No Jay, he's a new face. He was just trying to stop the Monster Twins."

The voice moves in front of me and after one look I wish he'd stayed where he was.

I'll be having nightmares about that face for a week.

He could get a job as the villain in a Kung Fu film any time he wanted and I bet he can fight as well.

Then he smiles.

It's not much better but as least I stop wanting to wet myself.

"Thanks for that mate."

I decide to start breathing again.

"Good to know someone stands up for us. I reckon that makes you a friend. Anyone gives you grief, tell them to come find Big Jay and I'll sort them out."

My turn to nod now; my throat is suddenly too dry to speak.

His phone beeps.

"Time I was gone," he says. "People to see."

Somewhere a school bell starts to ring as well.

I'm going to be late on my first day.

Great start Jamie.

The girl starts running, shouting "Thanks Jay!" over her shoulder.

"Yeah, thanks," I manage before deciding to try and catch her up.

Big Jay's got the sort of face you want to run away from.

My new name

Red's fast but I catch up as she slows to walk through the school gates.

"So, you the Red Sock Ninja then?" she asks.

I must have looked blank.

"You do know you're wearing one red sock and one green one don't you?"

I've done it again.

Sometimes I think so hard that I forget what I'm supposed to be doing. I'd been so worried about school that I must have picked up one of yesterday's socks.

"Come on," she says. "I suppose we'd better go to the office and tell them you're here."

How does she know I'm new?

She seems to find her way around the place which is good because I haven't got a clue. I'm joining the school halfway through the term and not looking forward to it one bit.

The woman in the office takes me to see the Head and Red disappears.

The Head is called Mrs Wallace and she seems ok.

Her desk looks like someone's emptied a rubbish bin over it and her phone keeps ringing so I guess she's sort of busy.

She says hello and welcome to the school and that sort of thing between the phone calls. Then she gives up and just takes me to my new class. I think she's glad to get out of her office.

I'm in Year 4 and my new teacher is Miss something or other. It sounds like "Smart Ink" or "Smurf Ting" but I'm not sure.

Her name's written on the classroom door but I'm not too good at reading and some of the letters don't seem to go together or sound out anything I remember.

Luckily everyone calls her Miss S, so I decide to do the same.

She pairs me up with a boy called William and tells him to look after me and show me where everything is. She even gives us ten minutes out of the class to wander around.

"This is our classroom."

Well, I know that already.

"And this is the other class in Year 4. Year 3 are over there," he waves in a general direction, "and Years 5 and 6 are round the corner."

So far so good. I think I can remember that.

We walk down the corridor as the tour continues.

"Toilets are down there. Smells a bit but you'll get used to it. Wally tends to wee on the floor if he gets distracted so don't talk to him in there unless you want to get wet."

Must try to remember that.

Wonder who Wally is?

"Mrs Wallace's office is there, she's the Head."

I already know that as well.

"And there's Mr Jenson's office. He's the deputy and runs the football team. Says we're going to win the Cup this year. First time ever."

Do I look as though I'm interested in football?

Billy, as he says he's called, gives me the full tour and it doesn't get any better. I'm glad to be back in the classroom even if we're about to start Literacy.

Well I suppose it's best that Miss S finds out right away how useless I am.

I try, but the letters never want to stick in my head.

I'm not thick or anything. I just have problems reading.

I can add up and stuff but sometimes I can't read the questions properly so I get things wrong in Maths as well.

Maybe you can see now why I'm not so keen on school these days.

"Jamie," says Miss S, "why don't you come over here and read to me

while the rest of the class start
their worksheets."

My day's going from bad to worse
and it's not even lunchtime yet.

A surprise

Reading to Miss S isn't too bad after all.

She takes it slowly and doesn't worry when I make a mistake. Well, more than one mistake.

Ok, lots of mistakes.

"I like my class to make mistakes," she says. "That's how we learn. Mistakes tell me where I've got to teach you some more. They tell me when I'm getting things wrong."

Never knew that teachers got stuff wrong.

Ok, I knew it happened but I'd never known a teacher who admitted it. Maybe I could fit in here after all.

The rest of the morning goes alright and then it's lunchtime.

That's when I realise Billy hadn't told me where we go for lunch and that's why I'm late.

"Hurry up boy," shouts the teacher at me, "stop being so slow!"

I'm not being slow on purpose but now doesn't seem a good time to say so.

There's an empty space next to some tall kid, so I quickly sit down.

"Hello," he says, "I'm Wally."

Now I know why there's the empty chair. Good job it's the hall and not the toilets.

Turns out he's ok. We chat about stuff and he tells me who's who.

The shouty teacher is Mr Jenson and he seems to hate everyone except his football team. They can get away with murder according to Wally.

Football is a big thing at the moment because our school is heading towards some Cup Final or something for the first time. Seems we don't win much these days and Mrs Wallace is quite excited about it.

The other big thing I learn is to avoid the Pikes.

They're this big family from the estate and all of them come to this school. Brothers, sisters, cousins, second cousins. You name it, they all come here. Them and their mates.

Then there's the other estate gang to avoid which seems to be made up of everyone who hates the Pikes.

In between these two gangs are the rest of us. I say us, because I'm not a Pike and as I don't know any Pikes I can't hate them yet can I?

So I guess I'm stuck in the middle and will have to avoid both gangs just like everyone else.

After lunch we go out to play and that's when it all gets interesting.

I see a few people from my new class and we start chatting. They want to know all about me and I want to tell them as little as possible. My life's like that at the moment.

Then Red comes up to say hello and everything changes.

Most of my new friends suddenly find somewhere else they'd rather be and drift away. That leaves just me and Wally standing there.

"This is Red," I say to Wally, pleased that I know at least one person outside of my class.

"I know," he says. "Everyone knows Red Pike."

Well I don't.

Well I do, but I didn't know she was a Pike and I didn't know what that name meant until lunchtime.

Now I'm able to work out a few things.

Wally had told me that all the gang members were a bit scary but the worst of the lot was a grown up cousin.

What he hadn't told me was the cousin's name but I think I can figure it out.

I think this cousin's the one who called me mate and said I was their friend.

Guess I'm in a gang after all and didn't even know I'd joined.

Wally decides that now would be a good time to go find the toilets.

Wish I could join him.

I think I'd rather risk a shower than what might happen next. I can see some of Red's mates lurking in the background and they look scary.

How to win at football

I feel like a Ninja suddenly faced with all of his enemies at once and finding that he's left his sword under his bed with his missing green sock.

Just then the bell goes and everyone starts moving at once, all in a hurry to line up with their class.

Red grins at me.

"Laters!" she says and runs off.

She's good at running off.

It takes me a while to get my feet moving again which is good because I'm not sure where my class line up.

Lucky thing Wally's so tall. He stands out like a lighthouse and I'm able to find the right line to join.

This afternoon is a bit special as our class is playing football against the school team to give them a bit of a warm up before the coming Cup match.

Nobody told me or Mum about any of this so I don't have a kit to wear which is fine by me as I hate football anyway.

Miss S says it's ok and not to worry as I can watch with the girls.

It seems to be one of those schools where the girls play netball and the boys play football. I think I'd rather play netball; that's how much I hate football.

You know I said that I didn't know anyone else in the school except for Red?

Turns out I'm wrong.

There on the football field is Mr Chubby and the Joker, my friends from this morning. They both scowl at me and I grin back knowing that I'm safe while Big Jay is still lurking in their minds.

Mr Jenson is refereeing the match and as usual he's shouting at everyone except his team. My class are too slow in getting changed, too slow in sorting themselves out and too slow in everything in the universe except for annoying Mr Jenson.

I don't think he's being fair but that's before the match kicks off. Then I know he's not being fair. I also know why and how our school team has got so far in this competition.

Some of my classmates are quite good but they don't stand a chance. The Year 6 boys are bigger and stronger and don't mind shoving their weight around. Some of our guys go flying but the ref doesn't do anything about it until we try to do the same thing back to them.

Suddenly Mr Jenson remembers the rules and awards his team a free kick right in front of me on the sideline. Their striker picks up the ball and places it about three metres closer to our goal and away from the touchline.

He's cheating and nobody seems to care.

He isn't the only one cheating either. My two bully friends are defenders which means that they flatten anyone who comes near them. Their idea of tackling is to ignore the ball and throw their feet at the legs of any of our players to bring him down.

Even I know that's illegal but Mr Jenson seems to have trouble noticing. He's far too keen on watching our side for anything they might do wrong so he can blow his whistle and award his team a free kick.

By the end of the lesson, our side is five goals down and two of our players have been taken to the nurse's room.

No wonder the school team is doing so well. They're cheating their way to the final with the help of a blind referee called Mr Jenson.

Peter Marney

The babysitter from hell

The rest of the week goes by quickly and suddenly it's Friday night.

I've been looking forward to a night in with Mum when she isn't too tired to chat but she's got other ideas. Seems she's been invited out with the girls from work and I'm to have a babysitter.

I remind Mum that I'm 9 years old so she changes the name to "Big boy sitter" which sounds even worse.

I go to answer the doorbell when it rings as Mum's still busy getting ready and that's when I trip through a time warp.

We seem to have skipped forward about six months and it's suddenly Halloween. Well, someone is dressed for "Trick or Treating" anyway.

The ghoul on the doorstep tells me her name is Keira and that she's looking after me tonight. At least she doesn't ask about my blood group. Maybe she's not fussy and drinks the blood of anything.

As Mum's shouting I guess I'll have to let Keira in.

It's going to be a fun night.

Mum dashes down the stairs and leaves me with a kiss and a cloud of perfume. I'm to be a good boy for Keira and go to bed without a fuss at nine o'clock. She's forgotten how old I am again.

So there's me and Keira staring at each other over the coffee table.

"There's a saying that you don't judge a book by its cover," she says.

"What?" I reply.

Did I tell you how good I am at chatting?

"It means that what you see isn't always what you think it is."

She looks me up and down.

"Take you for instance."

I'd rather she didn't.

"You look like a dorky 8 year old boy."

"Nine," I say.

I told you I was good at chatting.

"A dorky 9 year old boy then. But I could be wrong. Maybe you're a Superhero in hiding. Maybe sometimes you wear your red knickers over your blue pyjamas and fly to the rescue of stranded dogs."

How did she know I had blue pyjamas?

"Or maybe you tie your black joggers around your head and become a secret ninja."

Has she got a camera in my bedroom?

Time to start talking before she shares any more of my secrets.

"Shall I tell you what I see?" I ask, eager to get some revenge.

"No," she says, "let me guess what you think you see. I can read minds you know."

Well, all witches can do that.

"You see a teenage girl with long blonde hair and too much black eye shadow. You see her baggy black t-shirt with black leggings and black pumps. In short, you see a Geek, a Goth, an Emo."

Maybe I do.

I've no idea what half those words mean.

"What you don't see is my skills in Kung Fu or all of the books I've read and films I've seen. You tell me any film you've watched and I can tell you the plot."

This is good to know because I've just lost the plot and I've no idea what this girl is on about.

I say the first film that comes into my head.

She's clearly impressed.

"I said film, not baby cartoon."

So I fire off about four titles I'd watched with Dad and she comes back with the plot for every single one of them. She knows the names of all the characters, what they did in the film and why.

She tells me stuff about those films which even Dad didn't know.

"Have you ever wondered why the villains all queue up to fight the hero instead of steaming in all at once?" she asks.

I'd always worried about that with these films and decided it was because we'd get fed up if the hero always died in his first fight.

"Two or more people try to fight you at once, they can get in each other's way. A good fighter can use that and get his enemies to start hitting each other."

I stand up.

"What do girls know about fighting?" I say.

I wish I'd kept my mouth shut.

She stands up as well and hits me twice; once in each arm.

Babysitters aren't supposed to do that are they?

Suddenly I can't move. My arms have gone all dead.

"Now you've got two choices," she says. "Either you can go crying to your Mummy when she comes back or I can teach you how to do that."

What sort of choice is that?

Peter Marney

Ninja training

For the next few weeks I try to become invisible.

Most of my classmates don't want to know me now they think I'm a Pike, even though I've tried to keep away from both gangs.

The word's gone through the rest of the school as well and so I'm

left pretty much alone apart from
Wally and Red.

Although she's a Pike, Red isn't
part of the gang either, and tries
to stay out of all that which suits
me fine. No way do I want to get
between the gangs, either in school
or on the estate.

Red tells me she's fed up with
always being blamed for something
someone else in her family has
done. She also tries to tell me
that Big Jay isn't as bad as people
say but I'm not sure. I still
remember that face.

Meanwhile Miss S is teaching me
things during the day and Keira's
teaching me things twice a week
when she comes babysitting.

Ok, it's not the right word but
what am I supposed to say?

Superhero sit?

Ninja sit?

You see the problem, don't you?

Anyway, I don't own a cape so I'm not a superhero and Keira's busy proving that I'm not a ninja either.

"First rule of being a ninja," she says, "is don't be one."

Ok, I'm confused already.

"You've got to be the last one anybody suspects of being a ninja. Like in the films. The hero is always pretending to be a servant or a lowly wanderer. He doesn't come into town making a big noise does he?"

I shake my head.

"No, he slides in unnoticed. He stays unnoticed until he's killed off all the bad guys."

I wonder if I can get away with killing Mr Jenson?

Maybe not.

He is one of the bad guys though. The more I see of him, the more I'm sure of it.

Even Wally doesn't like him.

"He made me stand outside the staffroom just because I was late for break and running down the corridor," Wally told me, "and I could hear him inside."

"Why do we keep bothering with the thick ones?" he said. "They're still going to be thick. Why should I waste my time?"

That's what Wally said he'd overheard and I trust Wally even though I won't stand next to him in the toilets.

I suppose being thick includes not being able to read properly, so I guess Mr Jenson wants to write me off as well. As I said, he's one of the bad guys.

He also lets his football team cheat and that can't be right can it?

I mean, what's the point of winning if you have to cheat?

They are winning though.

After last week's match they're now in the semi finals.

Maybe our school might just win something for the first time ever.

Peter Marney

Do not try this at home

Something's different in school this morning, I can feel it.

There's a tension everywhere.

The playground before bell is unusually quiet and nobody's playing anything. Everyone's just standing around looking at each other.

No, not looking.

Glaring.

As soon as I walk in, Wally's by my side.

"Have you heard?" he asks.

No, I haven't heard but I'm guessing that it's something serious.

"Someone got stabbed last night on the estate. They reckon Big Jay done it."

The mysterious "They".

Kiera's told me about "They".

Every time something nasty happens, people start talking about "They".

"They say all the kids on the estate are tearaways."

"They say that girls shouldn't play football."

Now "They" were saying that Big Jay has knifed someone. But when I wander around the playground and start asking people, nobody has seen anything and it's all just gossip.

Both gangs are blaming each other and looking for a reason to start a fight.

All it needs is for some clown to give them an excuse.

Enter Mr Jenson.

"I want the lot of you in the hall now!" he shouts.

A please would be nice but that's not his way.

When he gets us in there, he puts all the Pikes on one side and the rest of us on the other. Then he starts shouting at them.

"Just because one of you Pike's gone and knifed some innocent guy doesn't mean that you can drag your stupid estate wars into my school. Nothing is going to stop my football team from winning this cup and if that means throwing some of you out of school then that's what's going to happen. Do you Understand?"

Nobody moves.

He turns to us.

"So if any of you see any Pike causing trouble I want you to come straight to me and let me sort it out, right?"

Like that's going to happen.

Nobody likes Mr Jenson apart from his team and half of them are only there because he's bullied them into not quitting. We've all suffered his shouting and his cheating and know it's not fair.

Not even the worst of the Pike's enemies are going to talk to Mr Jenson.

That's how my day started and it didn't get any better.

It was like walking on thin ice. Everybody was scared to even breathe and suddenly we're all being super polite to each other.

Nobody wants to be the cause of a fight today.

I'm glad to get home in one piece and tell Keira all about it that evening.

"Lots of lessons to be learned from this, ninja boy," she says, walking into the kitchen.

She picks up one of the knives that Mum kept from when she used to cook. It's the big sharp one which I've been told never to touch.

Kiera starts flashing it about.

"A thing like this is dangerous," she says.

I know that already and waving it about isn't making it any less dangerous.

"You see, it's like a ninja sword. It can kill people. Doesn't have to be much. A small cut in the wrong place and you can bleed to death in minutes."

That's nice to know.

She slides the blade back into the knife block and I start breathing again.

"That's why everyone was being super polite. Nobody wants to get in a fight which might spill out of school and into something serious."

I see what she's getting at.

"The best way to win a fight is not to get into one in the first place. There's lots of ways to win without knocking people down," she says.

Ok, not so sure about this one but I'll let her keep talking.

"Next lesson, never enter a bum kicking contest against a porcupine."

"A what?" I ask.

I know the Tiger Stance and the Fighting Crane from the Kung Fu films but I've never seen the Porcupine.

"Think of a hedgehog but with enormous prickles. Actually,

they're more like spikes. That's a porcupine."

I have an image of a giant hedgehog trying to stand on two legs so it can kick me on the bum.

Keira isn't amused.

"The thing is, even if you get to kick first, you're still going to end up with a leg full of spikes. A clever ninja chooses his battles. Never fight a porcupine."

She looks back at the knife block.

If she's going to start waving that thing around again then I'm going to go and hide somewhere.

"If someone is much more powerful than you, then they'll always win. Walk away and live to fight another day."

I suddenly realise what she's talking about.

"Mr Jenson's the porcupine isn't he?"

She smiles.

"He's a teacher so, whatever we do, we're always going to be in the wrong. We're always going to lose."

Sometimes I can be quite clever you know.

It still isn't right though.

"Stop thinking battles and start thinking tactics. That's the sign of a skilful ninja."

I try to get Keira to tell me what to do but she's decided not to play that game.

"Your school, your life, and your problem, ninja boy. Just be skilful."

Sometimes I hate being the Red Sock Ninja.

Wally starts thinking

By Monday morning things have become a bit clearer.

Turns out the innocent guy who'd got himself stabbed isn't so innocent after all and is well known as a local criminal.

Big Jay was picked up by the police but they'd had to let him go as he'd been helping out down the youth club when the guy got stabbed and so couldn't have done it. Youth club?

That doesn't sound like the sort of thing Big Jay would be doing of an evening but what do I know? Thinking about it, all I know about Jay is from what "They" say.

The whole stabbing thing turns out to be a fight between criminals and none of the estate were involved at all so we can all calm down again.

School's much more relaxed this morning until we get the news.

Our team has won their last match and are through to the Cup Final which is to be held on our playing field on Friday afternoon. Best of all, the whole school can go to watch and cheer them on.

How excited am I?

No way I'm going to be cheering for a load of cheats, even if they're wearing the school colours, and nobody's going to make me!

The other great news is that, on Friday morning, all the Juniors have to sit some big test.

Wonderful!

Something else for me to struggle to read and mess up.

What a great week this is turning into.

At lunchtime I find Red and Wally and tell them about Keira and the porcupine.

Red has taken to calling us the Red Sock Ninja Clan and we've sort of become friends.

We laugh at the idea of a bum kicking contest but Wally doesn't join in. He's got that far away look which means he's thinking.

We could be here for some time.

Peter Marney

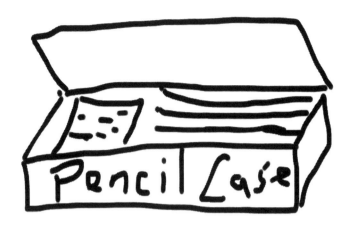

My little helper

Suddenly Friday's here and there we are, sitting down and taking the test.

Miss S has read out the rules and made sure we all understand them.

No talking, no getting up and wandering around, silent working only.

What a fun morning this is going to be.

Lucky for me, I've found a way to make things a bit easier.

I've put a little bit of paper in my pencil box with some of the words I have trouble spelling written on it and some of the tricky times tables. That should help a bit.

Miss wanders about for a while so I keep the lid closed until she's back at her desk and doing some marking. Then I ease the pencil case open and start to answer the questions.

Suddenly Wally sticks up his hand.

"Please Miss, Jamie's cheating!"

I shut the lid quickly and try to look innocent.

Nice to know who your friends are.

Miss S looks shocked.

"Is this true Jamie?" she asks me.

"Of course not," I say.

"He's lying Miss."

Thanks Wally.

"Look in his pencil case Miss."

She does and I'm in trouble.

"Jamie, I'm very disappointed in you. It's not like you to cheat."

"Cheating's wrong isn't it Miss?"

Shut up Wally, you're supposed to be on my side.

"Yes, it is Wally and I don't expect any of you to do something so naughty, especially not you Jamie."

"Bad kids get sent to Mrs Wallace don't they Miss?"

Me and Wally are going to have a very interesting chat later on. For now I just glare at him.

Anyway, what with Wally winding up Miss S and everything, I end up getting sent to Mrs Wallace.

Turns out I'm not the only one caught cheating.

What a surprise that is.

Not.

The door opens and both of us get marched in. Someone has already told Mrs Wallace what's happened and she's not happy.

"Cheating is one of the worst things any pupil of this school can do," she says.

"Jamie, I'm shocked that you'd do such a thing and the same goes for you Kylie."

Kylie starts crying.

Time for me to try and get out of this mess.

"I'm sorry Mrs Wallace. It's just that me and tests don't get on. I know cheating's wrong and it was stupid of me to do it. Nobody should cheat should they."

Mrs Wallace agrees. It's against the ethics of the school, whatever ethics are; I don't think now's a good time to ask.

"Now promise me, both of you, that you will never cheat again."

Kylie stops crying and speaks up.

"Please Miss, if we're promising, can you promise something too? Can you promise to come and watch the Cup Final this afternoon?"

This school's going football mad.

Fancy asking that when you're being told off.

Mrs Wallace is a very busy lady but Kylie makes her promise that she'll come and watch some of the match at least. Then the phone rings again and we're sent back to class.

I look across at the sniffing girl.

"Kylie?"

Red grins.

"Yeah, Mum's rubbish at choosing names."

Peter Marney

Cheating

It's funny how quickly ideas spread through a school.

The news of our cheating flew around the playground and soon everyone is saying how wrong it is to cheat.

Then someone asks, "So if cheating's wrong, why are we supposed to cheer for our football team? We all know they're a bunch of cheats."

I think that someone was Wally but I could be mistaken. These Red Sock Ninjas all sound alike to me.

Anyway, come the afternoon, we're all surrounding the football pitch with some of the other school's supporters lined up along one side as well.

Turn's out the match might be fairer than we're expecting because, as it's our pitch, the other school supplies the referee.

I won't bore you with the details but the game's pretty rubbish up to half time. We've been done for a few fouls and the Monster twins are warned for some very iffy tackles but nobody's scored yet.

Mr Jenson is one of the linesmen and flags the other side a few times for some odd stuff which only he seems to notice. Other than that, he's strangely quiet.

He isn't the only one being quiet
either.

Nobody is really cheering
anything.

Come the second half, things liven
up a bit.

The other side score and their
supporters make some noise. Some of
our lot join in which doesn't go
down too well with Mr Jenson.

That goal must have cheered up the
other side because they're soon
attacking again and running towards
our penalty area. Suddenly one of
the Monster Twins collides with the
referee and the teacher goes down
holding his ankle.

I happen to look over at Mr Jenson
at that moment and, for some
reason, he's grinning. That doesn't
seem right.

Then I begin to understand.

With the ref unable to continue
the game, Mr Jenson has to take

over. Now isn't that a fortunate accident?

Monster boy doesn't get sent off either.

Strange that.

From then on, things take their usual course and we start to get all of the decisions going in our favour. The other team are good though and with a minute to go, they still lead one goal to nil.

They're on the attack coming down my side of the pitch. Their player is just about to cross the ball to the middle when a well known pair of monster feet sweep his legs out from under him. The other side stop for the foul but our lads know better.

They keep playing as they know for certain that Mr Jenson is never going to blow the whistle against them. The ball gets moved quickly up field and then passed to our centre forward who's well offside but who scores anyway.

Their linesman puts his flag up but before anyone can complain, Mr Jenson blows the final whistle and herds our team back to the sidelines.

The other teacher comes storming over but it's too late. Mr Jenson says he's sorry for not spotting the flag but he's blown his whistle and the game's over. Too late to do anything about it and it's now down to penalties.

Their teacher's not happy and hurries back to his team.

That's when Mr Jenson turns on us lot.

"Where's all the cheering then? You're here to support the school team and I want the lot of you to cheer, understand?"

I turn to Miss S who is standing next to me. I must have forgotten how close she was because I think I spoke rather loudly.

"Cheating's wrong isn't it Miss? That tackle was a foul and we were well offside."

The other kids mutter their agreement and I can hear Red's voice amongst them.

"So, if our team's cheating, we shouldn't be cheering them should we Miss?" I ask.

"No Jamie, we shouldn't," says Miss S, right on cue.

For some reason this makes Mr Jenson suddenly very angry.

Nobody's going to tell him what he can and can't do with his football team especially not some young teacher hardly out of school herself. It's his school and if he wants to order us to cheer then cheer we will or the whole lot of us will be in detention, me especially.

Have I mentioned that Mr Jenson doesn't like me?

Suddenly a voice comes from the back of the crowd.

"I'm sorry Mr Jenson but this isn't your school. I believe it's mine and I think that Jamie has a point."

It's Mrs Wallace.

"I've been watching the match and I'm ashamed that our football team can behave so badly. They've been cheating the whole of the second half and you've not been stopping them. If this is how we got to the final then we don't deserve to be here."

Mr Jenson is going bright red.

"I will not be spoken to like this in front of the whole school," he shouts.

"I agree," says Mrs Wallace. "Go and get changed and wait in my office. There's going to be a few changes made in this school starting now. I'm taking over as the team coach until we can find someone more suitable.

I've been spending far too much time in my office and that needs to stop. Perhaps I need a deputy who does all of my paperwork full time."

That doesn't sound like a fun job and Mr Jenson doesn't look too impressed. He storms off back to the building to await his telling off.

Meanwhile Mrs Wallace gathers the team around her.

"I'm afraid that some of you won't be playing for the school team any more," she says.

I think I can guess who she's talking about.

"The rest of you, well, we'll have to see about that later. For now, I want to talk to the captain and our goalkeeper please."

In all the excitement I've forgotten that the game isn't over yet.

We still have to do a penalty shoot out to decide who wins the cup.

Maybe I'm getting a bit interested in football after all.

Peter Marney

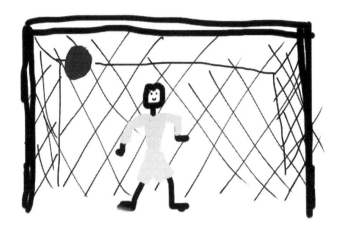

Penalties

Our keeper is standing perfectly still on his goal line as their striker places the ball on the penalty spot and takes a few steps backwards.

Then he's running and shooting and the ball flies straight into the back of the net.

Our keeper hasn't moved a muscle.

Their fans erupt in cheers but we're totally silent.

One nil to them.

Now it's our turn and the goalkeepers swap over.

Our captain takes the ball, places it on the spot and takes four strides backwards.

Even the birds have stopped singing.

Total silence.

Then slowly he walks forward, turns towards the corner flag and kicks the ball off the field.

It takes me a moment to understand what's just happened but then I'm up on my feet and cheering like mad. Red and Wally do the same and soon the whole school's joining in.

We're not cheering because we've lost the game; we're cheering because, for the first time this season, our team has done the right thing.

They're all surrounded by our fans and both our captain and goalkeeper are mobbed by their cheering classmates.

Mrs Wallace gets to present the Cup to the other side and the whole place erupts into even more cheering. The other side look a bit shocked but their teacher is grinning like a cat.

He's so pleased that he says he won't be reporting us and he'll allow Mrs Wallace to sort things out.

On the way back into school, Miss S starts looking at me with a frown on her face.

"It's all turned out rather well hasn't it Jamie."

"Yes Miss," I agree.

"Funny how cheating suddenly became top of everyone's mind isn't it."

I agree again.

"You and your friends haven't been up to something have you?"

I've told you that Miss S is a bit clever haven't I?

Well, maybe I'd forgotten to mention it but she is a bit clever. Very clever in fact.

Not as clever as the Red Sock Ninja Clan though.

As Wally figured out, sometimes you've just got to find yourself a bigger porcupine.

The End

The next book in the series

What with a mad dog, an oddly familiar school judo teacher and a secret door that Jamie didn't know existed, life is getting interesting for the original Red Sock Ninja.

Join the Clan on this new adventure as they try to defeat the bad guys without getting arrested themselves.

Details of all books can be found on my website.

www.petermarney.com

Peter Marney

About the author

Peter Marney lives by the sea, is just as bad at drawing as Jamie, and falls over if his socks don't have the right day of the week written on them.

On a more serious note, Peter has worked supporting children with reading difficulties and understands some of their problems. He is passionate about the importance of both reading and storytelling to the growing mind.

Peter Marney

The Red Sock Ninja Clan Adventures

Birth of a Ninja

Jamie's about to start another new school and has been told to stay out of trouble. Like that's going to happen!

It's not as if he wants to fight but you've got to help out if a girl's being picked on, right? Even if it does turn out that she's the best fighter in the school and laughs at your odd socks.

Follow Jamie as he makes friends, sorts out a big problem at his school, and discovers that his weird new babysitter knows secret ninja skills.

Hide and Seek

Find out why Jamie hates dogs and why he's hiding in a school cupboard in the dark. Has it got something to do with Keira's new training games for the Red Sock Ninjas?

The Mystery Intruder

Someone is playing in school after dark and it's not just the Red Sock Ninjas. Maybe Harry knows who it is but he's not talking so Jamie will have to find another way to solve this mystery.

The Mighty Porcupine

What do you do when your enemy is too powerful to fight? Has somebody finally beaten the Red Sock Ninjas?

The Mystery Troublemakers

Someone wants to get Jamie's new youth club into trouble but why? Maybe the Red Sock Ninjas can find the answer by climbing rooftops or will it just get them into more trouble?

Statty Sticks

Why is Jamie being attacked by a small girl who isn't Red and why does he get the feeling that someone is spying on him?

Has it got anything to do with why his school is in danger and how numbers can lie?

Enemies and Friends

Why has Jamie got a new uncle and why does everyone end up hiding in bushes?

Have the Red Sock Ninjas now found too big a porcupine and will it spell disaster for their future together?

Run Away Success

Where do you run to when everything goes wrong? That's the latest problem for the Red Sock Ninjas and this time Wally isn't around to mastermind the plan.

With the enemy closing in for capture, the friends must split up and disappear. Is this the end of the Clan or the beginning of a whole new experience for Jamie?

Rise and Shine

Why does going to the library get Jamie into a fight and what's that got to do with Keira's plan for getting rid of him?

Helping to put on a show with Miss G was difficult enough without guess who turning up. Yet again the Red Socks must use their skills to save the day and the show.

Rabbits and Spiders

Has Red set up Jamie on a date with Dog Girl? If so, why is he now running around in circles? Maybe it's got something to do with the fact that the enemy have at last found them again.

The Red Sock Ninjas must use all of their skills in this last